The F   Eg
& Sp

CW00866430

A first story about time

Written by Shen Roddie
Illustrated by Philip Norman

Pig was very excited. 'Duck! Duck! Come quickly!' he called out. 'What's up?' asked Duck.

'We've been chosen to run in the "Great Egg Race"'! said Pig.
'Don't be silly!' laughed Duck. 'You've never laid an egg in your life!'

'I don't have to lay an egg. I only
have to run with one in a spoon,'
snorted Pig. 'Oh, let's be a team,
Duck! It starts at one o'clock at the
Town Hall and ends at two o'clock.'

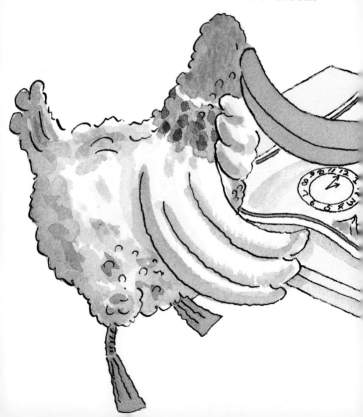

'How long do we have to run?' asked Duck.
'One hour,' answered Pig.
'How long is that?' asked Duck.
'Sixty minutes, Duck,' said Pig impatiently.
'How long's that?' asked Duck.

'As long as it takes to run through the town, past the fish shop, across the playground, over the bridge and back to town . . . with the egg still in the spoon, of course!'

'That's long!' cried Duck. 'Will
I have time to bake a cake?'
'Yes, but right now we have to
boil two eggs,' said Pig.

Pig put two eggs in boiling water and got the egg timer.
'Three minutes and our eggs
will be ready.'
'How long's a minute?' asked Duck.
'A minute is sixty seconds, Duck.'
'How long's a second, Pig?'
'As long as saying "one elephant"!
Try it!' said Pig.

Duck counted sixty elephants three times. By then the sand had run out of the egg timer. 'Time's up! They're ready!' Duck quacked. Pig and Duck lifted the eggs, grabbed two spoons and ran all the way to the Town Hall. They arrived just in time to hear the Town Hall clock strike one o'clock. BONG!

THE GREA

EGG RACE

A huge crowd had gathered to watch the race. Pig and Duck lined up beside Sheep and Dog and Mouse and Cat and Rabbit - all with their spoons and eggs.

Mr Cow, the starter, waved a flag.
Ten seconds to go. Duck counted
ten elephants to himself, then Mr
Cow yelled . . . 'GO!'

Duck leapt forward.
'Steady, Duck! You nearly dropped
your egg!' cried Pig.
'It's very wobbly!' wailed Duck.

Sheep and Dog whooshed past.
'Oh dear! They're ahead of us!' cried Pig.
'Better hurry, or they'll all finish before us!'

'Maybe not,' whispered Duck. 'Look behind!' Mouse, Cat and Rabbit had all dropped their eggs and were scrambling after them.

'Steady, Duck!' cried Pig. 'You
nearly dropped your egg again.'
'You're hurrying me too much!'
complained Duck.

Pig glanced back at the Town Hall clock.
'Good! We've only taken fifteen minutes.
That's a quarter of an hour. Plenty of time
to catch up with Sheep and Dog.'

Suddenly, Cat sailed past them.
'Oh no! Cat's overtaken us. That's
three faster than us! We have
no time to lose!
Speed up, Duck!'

'We've got to win!' squealed Pig.
'We've got to beat the clock!'
'You mean the clock is racing,
too?' asked Duck.

'Not exactly,' answered Pig.
'We have to get back before
the clock strikes two o'clock.'

'Let's go!' yelled Duck, flapping his wings in panic.

'FLYING IS NOT ALLOWED!' Mr Cow boomed over the loudspeaker.

The noise gave Duck such a fright that
PLOP! he dropped his egg.
'Now look what you've done!' moaned Pig.

'It's your fault!' said Duck. 'All this fast-slow, fast-slow makes me fidgety!'

'ANYONE DROPPING
AN EGG
MUST WAIT ONE
MINUTE!'
boomed Mr Cow.
'Oh dear!' sighed Pig.

'I remember,' smiled Duck proudly. 'That's sixty seconds. We have to count sixty elephants!' They picked up Duck's egg and counted sixty elephants.

When they reached sixty elephants, Pig
and Duck rushed off. They saw Cat was
galloping faster and faster. Suddenly,
she stopped, sniffed, then rushed into a
fish shop! 'Hooray!' puffed Pig. 'But
Sheep and Dog are still ahead of us!'

'Pig,' whispered Duck, 'I know how we can win this race! We'll cut through the woods. It's much shorter and more difficult, but it will take less time. Let's hope we finish before the others!'
'Good idea, Duck!' chuckled Pig.
'Let's go!'

'Follow me!' said Duck, leading Pig
off the road and into the dark woods.

It was so dark that Pig fell into a bog.

As he struggled out, Duck cried,
'Pig! Where's your egg?'
Pig shouted, 'Duck! Where's YOUR egg?'
'LOST!' they both wailed.

After what seemed like a very long
time (really only ten minutes), Duck
found his egg - just as it was walking
away (carried by Squirrel). Pig found
his in Robin's nest!

'Let's get back on the road!'
mumbled Duck.
'Yes, let's!' grunted Pig.
'We've wasted enough time!'

'I can see Mouse and Rabbit in front of us! There's no one else behind us! We're last!' wailed Duck.

'Don't give up, Duck! We've only been gone thirty minutes. That's half an hour. There's still time!' said Pig.

Mouse and Rabbit reached the playground. 'YIPPEE!' they yelled, jumping on to the swings. They meant to play for five minutes but were much longer.

'Time can go quickly,' giggled Mouse. 'I'm hungry.'

'So am I,' said Rabbit, and they picked up their eggs and ate them!

'That's two out of the race,' laughed Duck. 'Only Sheep and Dog are ahead of us,' panted Pig. Suddenly, someone shouted: 'CHEAT! CHEAT! Dog's egg is glued to the spoon!'

Dog was out of the race.

'This is our chance to win!' puffed Pig.
'We only have to beat Sheep.'

But suddenly, Sheep burst past them.
'I'm going to win! I'm going to win!'
she baahed. A spoon was sticking out
of her mouth. But there was no egg in it!
Sheep had lost her egg . . . and the race!

Balancing their eggs very carefully,
Duck and Pig sprinted to the finishing
line. 'Hurray! We've won!' they cried.

'And it isn't even two o'clock!'
'They did it in less than an hour!
A new record!' roared the crowd.
'That's the fastest egg race ever!'

But before you could say 'Superspooners!'
Pig and Duck were gone! Duck had
remembered the cake.

They both dashed home just in time.
'Delicious!' said Duck and Pig as they
ate it up in no time at all!

For Rebekah Judge . . . S.R.

First Edition published 1997 by Reader's Digest Children's Books,
King's Court, Parsonage Lane,
Bath BA1 1ER
Copyright © 1997 Reader's Digest® Children's Books,
a subsidiary of The Reader's Digest Association, Inc.

All rights reserved.
No part of this book may be reproduced,
stored in a retrieval system or transmitted
in any form or by any means,
electronic, electrostatic, magnetic tape,
mechanical, photocopying, recording or
otherwise, without permission in writing
from the publishers.

READER'S DIGEST®, THE DIGEST and
the Pegasus logo are registered trademarks of
The Reader's Digest Association, Inc.
of Pleasantville, New York, USA

Printed in China